OTHER YEARLING BOOKS YOU WILL ENJOY:

THE BEAST IN MS. ROONEY'S ROOM, *Patricia Reilly Giff*
FISH FACE, *Patricia Reilly Giff*
DECEMBER SECRETS, *Patricia Reilly Giff*
IN THE DINOSAUR'S PAW, *Patricia Reilly Giff*
THE VALENTINE STAR, *Patricia Reilly Giff*
THE SMALL POTATOES CLUB, *Harriet Ziefert*
THE SMALL POTATOES AND THE MAGIC SHOW, *Harriet Ziefert* and *Jon Ziefert*
LOST IN THE MUSEUM, *Miriam Cohen*
WHEN WILL I READ?, *Miriam Cohen*
FIRST GRADE TAKES A TEST, *Miriam Cohen*

YEARLING BOOKS/YOUNG YEARLINGS/YEARLING CLASSICS are designed especially to entertain and enlighten young people. Charles F. Reasoner, Professor Emeritus of Children's Literature and Reading, New York University, is consultant to this series.

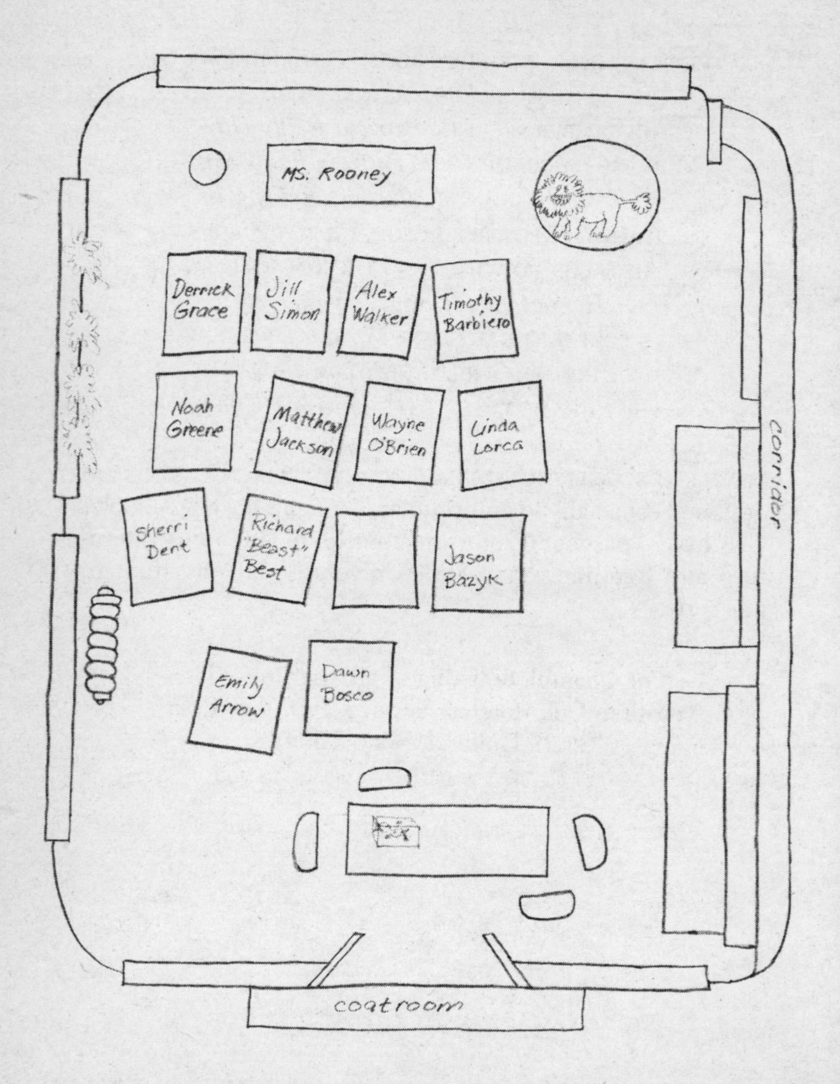

MS. Rooney
Derrick Grace
Jill Simon
Alex Walker
Timothy Barbiero
Noah Greene
Matthew Jackson
Wayne O'Brien
Linda Lorca
Sherri Dent
Richard "Beast" Best
Jason Bazyk
Emily Arrow
Dawn Bosco
corridor
coatroom

LAZY LIONS, LUCKY LAMBS

Patricia Reilly Giff

Illustrated by Blanche Sims

A YEARLING BOOK

Published by
Dell Publishing
a division of
The Bantam Doubleday Dell Publishing Group, Inc.
666 Fifth Avenue
New York, New York 10103

To the memory of Richard Flammer

ISBN: 0-440-44640-6

Printed in the United States of America

March 1985

10 9 8

CW

Chapter 1

Richard Best ducked behind the snow pile.

"I know you're there, Beast," Matthew yelled.

Richard dug at the snow.

He packed a clump into a snowball.

His hands were freezing.

He dashed up to the top of the pile. He tossed the snowball at Matthew Jackson.

It landed on top of Matthew's brown hat.

"Yeow," Matthew yelled.

Suddenly Richard remembered. They weren't supposed to play on the snow pile.

"Just wait till next time." Matthew grinned. "I'll make peanut butter out of you."

"Let's have a wrestling match," Richard said. "I'll be Battling Beast. You can be—"

The bell rang.

Beast looked back over his shoulder.

Everyone was lining up.

"I'll be . . ." Matthew stopped to think.

"Maybe we'd better get going," Beast said.

"Maybe," said Matthew.

He threw himself on top of Beast. "I'm Mad Dog Matthew Jackson," he yelled. "King of the wrestlers."

Matthew felt as heavy as a mountain, Richard thought. He had on a jacket and about four sweaters.

He smelled as if he had wet the bed last night.

Richard grunted.

He rolled over on top of Matthew.

"I can't believe this," a voice said. "Fighting. Rolling on the ground."

Richard looked up.

It was Mrs. Kettle, the strictest teacher in the school.

Richard scrambled off Matthew.

"Go straight to the principal's office," Mrs. Kettle said. "This minute."

Richard dusted the snow off his jeans.

He and Matthew started across the schoolyard.

Richard looked back once.

Mrs. Kettle was still staring at them.

"We're going to get killed," Richard said out of the corner of his mouth.

"Expelled, maybe," Matthew said.

"Maybe," Richard said.

He wondered where kids went when they got expelled.

Maybe they stayed home all the time, he thought.

Maybe they went to a special school. A school for expelled kids.

"Maybe we'll get left back," Matthew said.

"I hope not," said Richard. He had already been left back once.

He might never get out of Ms. Rooney's class.

He'd be doing the same stuff over and over again.

They passed Ms. Rooney's line.

It was a good thing Ms. Rooney was inside.

It was a good thing she didn't know they were going to the principal's office.

Everyone in the class was looking at them. Sherri Dent. Noah Greene.

Emily Arrow crossed her fingers. "Good luck."

Richard opened the big brown doors.

They went down the hall to the office.

"You first," Matthew said.

Richard opened the door.

Mrs. Lee, the secretary, was sitting at the front desk. She was typing.

The typewriter keys were clicking fast.

Mrs. Lee's fingers were bouncing up and down.

"We have to see Mr. Mancina," Richard said.

Mrs. Lee kept her eyes on the typewriter. "He's busy now," she said.

Richard looked at Matthew.

Matthew raised his shoulders in the air. "We'll come back some other time," he said.

"Right," said Richard.

Mrs. Lee frowned. "Sit down," she said.

Richard and Matthew sat in the visitors' chairs.

The typewriter keys kept clicking.

Once Mrs. Lee looked up. "What date is this?" she asked herself.

"February," said Matthew.

She shook her head. "No," she said. "It's March. March first."

Rat-tat-tat-tat-tat went the keys.

"March," said Mrs. Lee. "It comes in like a lion."

Richard opened his mouth.

He made believe he was roaring at Matthew.

Matthew made a roaring face back at him.

Then Richard remembered they were in trouble.

He closed his mouth again.

Mr. Mancina opened the inside door.

Richard could see he was wearing a purple tie.

The typewriter keys stopped clicking.

"I think we have two troublemakers here," said Mrs. Lee.

"Come into my office," said Mr. Mancina.

Richard stood up.

He could hear his heart begin to pound.

He hoped nobody else could hear it.

They went into Mr. Mancina's office.

Mr. Mancina had a McDonald's tray on his desk.

There was an Egg McMuffin on the tray.

Richard looked at Matthew.

He hoped Matthew had seen the Egg McMuffin.

Richard was surprised that a principal would go to McDonald's . . . just like a regular person.

Richard had never even thought about a principal eating before.

"What were you doing?" Mr. Mancina asked.

"Rolling . . ." began Matthew.

"The snow pile . . ." Richard began.

"Rolling in the snow?" Mr. Mancina asked.

"Near the snow pile," Richard said.

"I see," said Mr. Mancina.

"We're not going to do it anymore," Matthew said.

"No," said Richard.

"That's good," said Mr. Mancina. "I didn't think you were troublemakers."

Richard's heart stopped pounding.

"Do you know what month this is?" Mr. Mancina asked.

"It's March," said Matthew.

"March first," said Richard.

Mr. Mancina nodded. "Do you know what happens in March?"

Richard took a guess. "James Polk's birthday?"

Mr. Mancina shook his head. "No. It's the third marking period. It's report-card time again."

"Yes," Richard said. He swallowed a little.

He had forgotten all about report cards.

"I want to see good marks," Mr. Mancina said. "I know you can do it."

"I know we can," said Matthew.

Richard's heart began to pound again.

He had forgotten that report cards came in the middle of March.

‘‘All right, boys,’’ Mr. Mancina said. ‘‘Hurry back to Ms. Rooney’s room.’’

Richard and Matthew backed out the door.

Mrs. Lee’s fingers were still clicking.

‘‘Maybe I’ll get a good report card,’’ said Matthew.

‘‘Maybe,’’ Richard said.

He thought about being left back again.

He hoped he’d get a good report card too.

Chapter 2

Richard slid into his seat in back of Matthew.

Ms. Rooney looked up. "You're late today."

Richard ducked his head.

Ms. Rooney sighed. Then she said, "March comes in like a lion. It goes out like a lamb."

Richard pulled out his last piece of looseleaf.

He began to draw a lion face.

He put some fur on its forehead.

"Look outside," said Ms. Rooney.

Richard looked out the window.

Everything was gray and cold.

It was starting to snow again.

"What am I talking about?" Ms. Rooney asked.

Noah raised his hand. "You mean that the beginning of March is terrible. . . ."

"All snowy and windy," Emily Arrow said.

"Everybody gets colds," Jill Simon said. She sniffled a little.

"But the end of March is spring," said Alex Walker.

"Baseball," said Jason Bazyk.

"Sweaters," said Emily. "Flowers."

"Getting ready for my wedding," said Ms. Vincent, the student teacher.

"Everything soft like a lamb," said Linda Lorca.

Matthew turned around. "Baaa, baaa," he whispered.

"Baaa," Richard whispered back.

He yawned a little.

It looked like a blizzard outside, he thought. They'd never get to play baseball again.

In front of him Matthew slid down in his seat. "I'm sick of winter," he said.

Richard nodded. "Me too."

He put some fur on the lion's cheeks.

He drew in a big mouth and some fat teeth.

Matthew looked over his shoulder. "That's some lion."

"It's a March lion," Richard said.

"Is he yawning?" Matthew asked. "He looks as if he's falling asleep."

"He is not," Richard said. "He's getting ready to pounce on someone."

"Probably Mrs. Miller, the substitute teacher," said Matthew.

"Probably," said Richard.

"Did you two hear what I was saying?" asked Ms. Rooney.

"Yes," said Richard.

"No," said Matthew at the same time.

Ms. Rooney pushed at her puffy brown hair. "What was I saying?" she asked Richard.

"March comes in like a lion," said Richard.

Ms. Rooney looked surprised. "It's an exciting month," she said. "We'll do exciting things."

Richard sighed.

March was probably the worst month in the whole year.

Ms. Vincent went to the front of the room.

"Take out paper," said Ms. Rooney. "Ms. Vincent is going to do a lesson with you."

"Yes," said Ms. Vincent. "A writing project."

Richard drew a long skinny tail on his lion. He put a fat pom-pom on the end.

"Are you listening?" Ms. Vincent asked.

Richard nodded. "Hey, Matthew," he whispered. "Lend me some looseleaf?"

Matthew raised one shoulder. He held up a wrinkled piece of paper. "This is my only one."

Richard turned around. Maybe Emily . . .

"Settle down," said Ms. Rooney from the side.

"We're going to write stories," said Ms. Vincent. "They have to be finished by—"

"By March seventeenth," said Ms. Rooney. "By St. Patrick's Day."

"We're going to write true stories about real people," said Ms. Vincent.

"I'll write about James Polk," said Timothy Barbiero.

"Good," said Ms. Vincent. "Get lots of facts."

"Maybe I'll do Martin Luther King," Alex said.

"Neat," said Ms. Vincent.

Richard looked out the window.

He made believe he was thinking of someone to write about.

He looked at Ms. Rooney. She'd be mad as anything if she saw he had no looseleaf again.

He tore off a tiny corner of his lion paper.

He picked up his pencil and wrote:

Loos leef

He could see Ms. Rooney was looking out the window.

He tossed the piece of paper back at Emily's desk.

It landed on the floor between her desk and Dawn Bosco's.

Emily didn't even see it.

Ms. Rooney came a little closer.

She looked at the paper on his desk. "What's that?"

"It's a lion," Richard said.

"A lazy lion," said Matthew.

Ms. Rooney smiled a little. "This isn't drawing lions time."

Richard put his lion paper in his desk.

"Lazy lions are one thing," Ms. Rooney said. "Lazy boys are another. You'd better get to work."

"I don't have any more—" Richard began.

"Will someone please give Richard some paper," Ms. Rooney said.

Dawn Bosco leaned forward. "Here, Beast," she said. "You can have two pieces. It's special."

Richard looked at the paper.

It had two red hearts in the corner.

Just his luck, he thought. He had to use silly girls' paper.

"Is everyone ready?" asked Ms. Vincent.

"I think I'm going to write about Sally Ride," Emily said. "She's an astronaut."

"Terrific," said Ms. Vincent.

Richard raised his hand.

Ms. Vincent smiled at him.

"Does this count for the report card?" Richard asked.

"It certainly does," said Ms. Rooney.

Richard sighed. Writing stories was his worst subject.

If he got a bad mark in writing,maybe he'd be left back all over again.

He took out his pencil.

He put his heading on his paper.

There wasn't one person he could think of writing about.

He was going to have a terrible report card.

He knew it.

Chapter 3

It was Monday again. Richard looked out the classroom window.

It was beginning to snow. Huge white flakes.

They were covering the dirty snow.

"Oh, dear," said Ms. Rooney. "Half the class is asleep."

Richard made a little snoring noise.

Ms. Rooney frowned. Then she clapped her hands. "Let's get out of here."

Richard opened his eyes wide.

In front of him Matthew sat up straight.

"Great," said Ms. Vincent.

"Yes," said Ms. Rooney. "We'll go outside."

"In a blizzard?" Jill asked.

"Get your coats. First row first," said Ms. Rooney. "It's not a blizzard."

"It's freezing out there," said Sherri Dent.

"That wouldn't bother Sally Ride," said Emily. "It won't bother me."

"I'll be right back," Ms. Rooney said. "I don't want to hear a sound in here."

As soon as Ms. Rooney walked out the door, the first row ran for their jackets.

So did the second row.

Richard stood up. He gave Matthew a little poke.

A moment later Ms. Rooney came back.

She was carrying a big box. She had a pile of black paper. "The art teacher gave me these," she said.

Richard went to get his jacket.

A million kids were in the coatroom. They were bumping into each other.

Jackets and hats were on the floor.

Matthew was on the floor too.

He was looking for one of his boots.

Richard grabbed his jacket. He went back to his seat.

There was a piece of black paper on his desk.

There was a magnifying glass too.

"I don't have enough to go around," said Ms. Rooney. "You'll have to have partners."

"Me and Richard," Matthew said. He gave Richard a little push. "Right, Beast?"

Richard nodded. He looked at Matthew through the magnifying glass.

Matthew looked like a big blurry blob.

This was a terrific magnifying glass.

It was much better than the little one Matthew had given him for Christmas.

Besides, Matthew's had a crack in it.

The class lined up.

"We're going to catch snowflakes," said Ms. Rooney.

"You can't do that," said Noah. "They melt in your hand."

Ms. Rooney shook her head a little. "Catch them on the black paper. Then look at them through the magnifying glass."

Richard was looking at Emily's wool hat through the magnifying glass.

It looked yellow and puffy.

It looked a little dirty too.

"Are you paying attention, Richard?" asked Ms. Rooney.

Richard stopped looking at Emily's hat.

"You have to look hard at things sometimes," said Ms. Rooney.

"Like snowflakes," Emily Arrow said. She pulled her yellow hat down over her eyebrows.

"Yes," said Ms. Rooney. "Through the magnifying glass you'll see how they really look."

Richard leaned against the chalkboard. He wished Ms. Rooney would stop talking. He wished she would hurry.

He was dying of the heat in his jacket and mittens.

Ms. Rooney didn't hurry, though.

She kept telling them that things look different if you really pay attention to them.

Richard picked up a piece of chalk.

He scrunched down behind Matthew.

He made a pile of snowflake dots on the board.

At last Ms. Rooney marched them down the hall.

They passed the office.

Mr. Mancina was standing there. Today he was wearing a red-and-yellow tie.

He winked at Richard.

"You may hold the door," Ms. Rooney told Richard.

Richard pushed at the outside door.

He held it open until everyone was out.

Then he ran to get in his place.

The wind was blowing the snow all over the schoolyard.

It blew Ms. Vincent's pink scarf across her face.

It tore Dawn Bosco's hat off her head.

Emily and Dawn ran across the schoolyard after it.

After a moment Richard could hardly see them.

Richard held out his black paper.

Snowflakes fell all over it.

Matthew held up the magnifying glass.

"Here's a star," said Richard.

"This one looks like a spider web," said Matthew.

"And here's a diamond," said Richard.

"Ms. Rooney's right," Matthew said. "Everything is different when you look at it carefully."

The black paper blew out of Richard's hand.

It sailed across the yard.

Richard and Matthew dived after it.

Richard could feel the wind on his face.

His nose was freezing.

"Grab the paper, Matthew," he yelled.

The paper landed on the snow pile.

Richard looked back at Ms. Rooney.

"All right," she called. "Go get it."

They dashed up the side of the snow pile.

Richard reached for the paper.

Then he and Matthew slid down again.

They lay in back of the snow pile out of the wind.

The snow fell softly on Richard's face.

He closed his eyes.

He stuck out his tongue to catch a flake.

He thought about diamonds and stars and spider webs.

"Have you done any of your real-person story yet?" Matthew asked.

Richard thought about the paper with the red hearts. He shook his head.

It was getting dirty now.

He was still trying to think of someone.

He wished he could think of a terrific person.

He thought about his lion again.

He'd like to write about a lion tamer.

He could call his story "A Lion Tamer's Life."

He scrunched his eyes closed tighter. He thought about the lion racing around in the jungle.

It was racing after Mrs. Miller, the substitute teacher.

She'd be running as fast as she could. Running on her skinny legs.

Would the lion tamer save her?

Richard started to laugh. Too bad he didn't know any real lion tamers to write about.

"The class is lining up," said Matthew.

Richard stood up. He dusted the snow off his jacket.

He could never write a story like that.

He'd be in trouble for writing about a teacher being chased by a lion in a jungle.

But he'd have to think of something.

Something very soon.

Chapter 4

It was Thursday. Time for special-help reading.

Emily and Alex and Matthew walked down the hall.

Richard stopped to look at the picture of James K. Polk.

James looked as if he were going to fall asleep any minute.

Richard didn't blame him.

The Polk Street School was probably the most boring school in the whole world.

Richard wondered if he could walk all the way to Mrs. Paris's room with his eyes shut.

He leaned his shoulder against the wall.

He closed his eyes.

He inched his way down the hall.

He made believe he was in the middle of a

blizzard. The snowflakes were coming down fast.

They looked like spiderwebs and diamonds and stars.

He heard Mrs. Paris's door open and shut.

The other kids must be inside already.

He'd have to hurry a little.

He leaned his shoulder harder against the wall. He made believe he was going to push the wall right over. It would fall into the fifth-grade class.

A brick would bounce right off his sister Holly's head.

Suddenly the wall ended.

Richard fell into the open doorway of Room 110.

His eyes flew open.

"What's the matter with you?" shouted Mrs. Miller, the substitute teacher.

Richard could see Holly slide down in her seat.

She probably didn't want the teacher to know that she had a brother who fell into classrooms.

"I'm here on a message," Richard said. "A message for my sister Holly."

"Make it quick, young man," said Mrs. Miller. "You've just spoiled my whole social studies lesson."

Richard walked down the aisle.

He leaned over Holly's desk.

"I'm going to kill you someday," Holly told him.

Richard made believe he was whispering something.

"What did you say?" Holly asked.

"Nothing," he answered. "I'm making believe I'm on a message."

"Get out of here, Richard," said Holly. She looked over at her friend Joanne. "He's crazy."

Richard hurried out of the room.

He raced down the hall to Room 100.

Mrs. Paris was sitting at the round table.

Emily and Alex and Matthew were sitting there too.

"Where have you been, Richard?" Mrs. Paris asked.

"In Mrs. Miller's room," he answered.

"I hope you're not in trouble," said Mrs. Paris.

Richard shook his head a little. He opened his reader.

They were reading a story about a frog and a princess. It was a very boring story.

Richard hated it.

He looked at the picture of the frog.

He was the ugliest thing in the world.

The princess didn't look so hot either.

"What do you think is going to happen in this story?" Mrs. Paris asked the class.

"The frog is going to kiss the princess," Emily Arrow said.

"Smack, smack," said Matthew.

"Do you think she knows he's a prince?" asked Mrs. Paris.

"No," said Alex. "But I do. If you look at the picture you can almost see a little crown on his head."

Richard looked at the picture. He looked hard. He didn't almost see a crown on the frog's head. He saw a little leaf from the pond.

"It's only a leaf," said Richard.

"You have to look very hard," said Alex.

Richard crossed his eyes.

"Well," said Mrs. Paris. "If you think hard about the story, what could you guess?"

"I'd guess the frog was a prince," Emily said. "He was very kind to the princess."

Richard flipped through the pages to see what the next story was.

He hoped it was better than frogs and princesses.

He hoped it was about baseball or rockets or a mystery.

But the next story had a picture of a little girl.

She was wearing a coat with a hood.

It was a red hood.

There was a wolf in the corner.

He had long yellow teeth.

Richard slammed the book closed.

"Almost time to go," said Mrs. Paris.

She went to her desk. She opened the drawer and pulled out a bag of dried fruit. "Something to sweeten your day," she said.

Richard reached into the bag. He took out a pile of raisins. He put them all in his mouth at once.

Just then Mr. Mancina came into the room. He was wearing a green-striped sweater. He had a box in his arms.

"New books," he told Mrs. Paris.

"Thank goodness," said Mrs. Paris. "Richard and I are sick of frogs and princesses."

Richard opened his eyes wide. He wondered how Mrs. Paris knew.

Maybe she looked hard at things like Ms. Rooney.

Mr. Mancina winked at them. Then he went outside.

"Oh, Richard," Mrs. Paris said. "I gave the others a list. Here's one for you too."

Richard took the paper. It was the kind from the ditto machine. It had purple writing on it.

Richard put it up to his nose.

He loved the smell of it.

Mrs. Paris smiled. "It's not to eat, Richard. It's a list of things to bring next Tuesday. We're going to do a project."

Richard followed the others out the door.

He looked at the paper. It was all about kits.

He wondered what a kit was.

Maybe something like a box. Something to put your books in.

He looked at the list.

Old shirts and ties. String. Wrapping paper.

He thought about report cards.

He'd probably get an all-right mark in reading.

In math too.

Then he thought about his real-person project.

He was going to get an F.

He wished he could stay home until that was over.

He wished he could be sick.

He swallowed hard. Maybe he was getting a sore throat. Half the class had had sore throats last week.

Too bad he never got a cold.

He shoved the purple ditto paper into his pocket.

Then he stopped for a sip of water.

Matthew had stopped for water too.

"I've got some great pieces of wood," Matthew said. "I'll bring two for you."

Richard nodded.

He wondered what Matthew was talking about.

Just then Ms. Rooney stuck her head out the door.

"Hurry," she said.

Richard wiped his mouth on his sleeve.

He hoped they weren't going to work on their real-people story.

He couldn't even find the paper with the hearts on it anymore.

And he was just too tired to look for it.

Chapter 5

Richard opened the back door.

He dropped his books on the kitchen floor.

He poked at the fruit on the table.

Nothing but dead apples.

He wished his mother would buy the good red juicy kind instead of the ones with spots.

He opened the back door again.

"Where are you going?" Holly asked.

"Out," said Richard.

"You're supposed to stay in this week," Holly said, "until Mommy gets home from work."

Richard frowned. He had forgotten he was in trouble.

He had forgotten he had lassoed the blue statue. The one on the shelf in the living room.

He had forgotten it had broken into a million pieces.

He put on his mittens.

"Mommy said—" Holly began.

"That's all you know," Richard told her. "She said if I had to do something for school I could—"

"What do you have to do?" Holly asked. She put her hands on her hips.

Richard wished he could lasso her.

"I have to get some stuff."

"What stuff?" she asked.

"M.Y.O.B.," he said. "That means mind your own business."

"I know what it means," Holly said. "I'm supposed to be baby-sitting you. You have to tell me . . ."

Richard took some money off the counter. "I have to get some stuff from the candy store. We're making kits."

"Well, make sure it isn't candy," Holly said. "You're going to end up with rotten teeth."

Richard slammed out the door.

He put half his money in one mitten. He put the other half in his pocket.

That way he wouldn't lose his money all at once.

First he climbed on his old fort in front of the house.

He heard Holly banging on the window.

He jumped off the fort.

At the corner he could see a couple of kids having a snowball fight.

He thought about joining in. He looked back.

Holly was still looking out the window.

The big tattletale.

He went down the block to the candy store.

Inside, Emily and Jill were sitting at the counter. They were having double-dip chocolate cones.

"Want some?" Emily asked. "I had extra money. I cleaned the refrigerator for my mother. I put all the jars on one side. I put all the bottles on the other."

Richard shook his head.

"I'm trying to do what I'm supposed to," Emily said. "I'm practicing to be an astronaut like Sally Ride."

"How do you do that?" Richard asked.

"I do thirteen sit-ups every day. I study hard."

Richard looked around the store.

He didn't want to think about studying hard.

He didn't want to think about his real-person story.

"I'm doing a movie star," Jill said.

Emily jumped off the stool. "Are you here for wrapping-paper too?"

"Yes," he said.

He walked to the back of the store.

He looked through the packages of paper.

It was all stuff with flowers, or babies with no clothes.

Emily held up a package of rainbow paper. "Isn't this cute?"

Richard nodded.

He found some green-and-orange-striped paper.

Then he went back to the counter. He looked at some black plastic spiders in a jar.

They looked horrible.

He wished he had enough money to buy a couple.

He'd put one in Holly's bed.

And one in the bathtub.

Holly would scream and scream.

Maybe she'd run away and never come back.

He paid for the paper and walked outside.

Holly wouldn't run away, he thought.

She wasn't afraid of spiders.

"Who is your real-person story about?" Emily asked.

"I don't know," Richard said. He raised his shoulders in the air.

He waved good-bye to them.

On the way home he tried to think of someone for his story.

He wished he could think of someone exciting.

Too bad nothing exciting ever happened.

He thought about the spiders.

He wished he could write a story about them.

Real ones.

Giant size.

He'd call his story "Richard the Spider Boy."

This time Holly would be afraid.

She'd be standing on top of the couch.

She'd beg him to get rid of the spiders.

He'd wait until they had crawled all over the place.

Then he'd lasso them. They'd fall on the floor. They'd break into a zillion pieces.

Just the way the blue statue had.

Suddenly he remembered looseleaf.

He should have gotten some at the candy store.

He thought about going back.

It was too much trouble.

Holly was waiting at the front door for him.

"That's all you got?" she asked. "Some crummy orange-and-green paper?"

Richard went past her.
He threw his jacket and mittens on the chair.
He didn't want to write a story about Holly.
He didn't even want to think about her.

Chapter 6

After supper Richard went up to his bedroom.

He looked at the pile of books on the shelf.

Encyclopedias. Old ones.

His Aunt Terri had brought them over last summer. She said she didn't use them anymore.

Richard pulled one off the shelf.

Aunt Terri said you could find out anything from an encyclopedia.

He opened it.

It smelled like Aunt Terri's basement.

Holly poked her head in the door. "Why do you have your nose in that book?" she asked. "Are you crazy?"

Richard pulled his head out of the book.

He slammed the book on his bed. "Get out of my room," he said.

"Richard's smelling books," Holly sang. "Richard's smelling . . ."

"I'm going to get you," Richard said. He started toward the door.

Holly ran down the hall to her room.

"Richard can't read. He has to smell," Holly yelled.

"Shut up," Richard yelled.

His mother came to the stairs. "Will you two stop fighting." she said.

Richard went back into his room.

He looked at the encyclopedia.

It was the one that had all the *D*'s in it.

Good. *D* was a nice beginning letter.

He'd find a *D* person to write about.

A terrific *D* person.

He'd get the best report card in the class.

Mr. Mancina would be thrilled.

He opened the book.

D-o-n-i-z-e-t-t-i.

Richard had never heard of him.

He couldn't even say his name.

It was hard to read about what he had done.

Richard stared at the story a long time.

There was a picture of Donizetti on top of the page.

He had a mustache. His hair was flying all over the place.

Richard thought he'd try for someone else.

He flipped the pages backward.

Stephen Decatur.

Stephen's picture was even bigger than Donizetti's.

It was a terrific picture.

Steven was standing on a ship.

He was wearing skinny white pants.

He had a jacket with lots of gold strings.

Stephen looked important.

He must have done something famous.

Richard stood in front of his mirror.

He made believe he was standing on a ship.

He made a telescope with his hands.

"Watch out," he said in a deep voice. "I am Stephen D."

"Watch out," said a voice behind him. "You are a Froot Loop."

It was Holly.

Richard ran down the hall after her.

But Holly raced into the bathroom. She locked the door.

Richard went back into his bedroom.

Then he thought about the looseleaf. He poked his head out the door.

Holly was still in the bathroom.

Quickly he went into Holly's room.

"Mother," Holly was yelling. "Make Richard leave me alone."

"Richard," his mother called.

Richard looked around for the looseleaf.

Holly came out of the bathroom.

"Mother," she yelled. "Richard's in my room."

"I'm just looking for looseleaf," he said.

"Again?" Holly put her hands on her hips. "You never have anything."

"Just give me one piece," Richard said.

"I wouldn't even give you the holes in the looseleaf," Holly said. She started to laugh.

Richard went back into his bedroom.

He looked under the bed for some paper.

Then he looked in his dresser.

There was a crumpled-up piece under his pajamas. It had some writing on it.

He'd have to erase it.

He punched his pillow and sat down on it.

He leaned the paper on the encyclopedia. Then he pulled his pencil out of his pocket.

It had a terrible eraser.

It made the paper look black.

It was a good thing he had to erase only three lines.

After he finished erasing, he pulled the encyclopedia closer.

He wished he could read what it said.

He began to write.

Chapter 7

Richard walked down the street. He was carrying his father's old blue shirt.

He held the green-and-orange paper under one arm.

He held his Stephen D. paper under the other.

"Wait for me," Holly shouted. "You're not supposed to cross Linden Avenue alone."

Richard looked around. He hoped no one had heard her.

She always had to make him look like a baby.

The biggest baby in the Polk Street School.

After they had crossed Linden Avenue, he waited at the corner.

Emily and Jill would come in a minute.

He climbed on a snow pile.

It was beginning to melt.

He could feel his boots sinking in.

His socks were going to be soaked.

Richard waved his father's shirt around.

It looked like a flag.

He thought about being on a ship.

Stephen D.'s ship.

He wondered if it was an aircraft carrier.

He didn't think so.

Stephen probably lived in the olden days.

Richard thought about being the captain of a ship. He'd be waving planes in.

Hundreds of them.

Too bad he couldn't write that for his real-person story.

Richard Best was the best waver in of airplanes, he'd say. Richard was the captain.

Too bad it wasn't true.

Too bad everyone would laugh at him if he said that.

"Hey, Beast," Emily yelled.

Richard jumped off the snow pile.

His Stephen paper flew out of his hand.

It landed in the slush.

He picked it up with two fingers.

"Yucks," said Emily.

"Double yucks," said Jill.

"It was my real-person story," Richard said.

He waved the paper around in the air.

Drops of water rolled off the bottom.

"Maybe you could do it over," Emily said. "In the classroom."

Richard looked at the paper.

He could hardly see the writing.

"Who was your real person?" Jill asked.

"Stephen . . ." Richard began, and stopped.

"Stephen who?" Emily asked.

"Stephen I don't know," Richard said. "I forgot."

"How could you write about someone . . ." Jill began.

"And not know his last name?" Emily said.

Richard sighed. It would take forever to find that page in the *D* encyclopedia again.

"You're supposed to know all about him," Emily said.

"I copied him out of an encyclopedia," Richard said. "The words were hard. It took a long time."

Jill opened her mouth into a little O. "I don't think you're supposed to do that."

"Not the whole thing," said Emily.

Richard opened his two fingers.

His Stephen paper sailed into the slush again.

He was going to get the worst report card in the Polk Street School. He'd probably be left back again.

And all because of a real-person story.

"Let's go," Jill said. "I think we'll be late."

Richard walked behind Jill and Emily.

He felt angry at everything.

He even felt angry at Emily.

She was supposed to be his friend.

She wasn't supposed to tell him not to copy.

They went down the block toward school.

Matthew was standing on the top step. "Hey, Beast," he yelled. "Look what I've got." He waved a bunch of sticks in the air.

"Hi, Matthew," Richard said.

"I finished my real-person story," said Matthew. "It's a great one."

"Good," said Richard. He tried to look glad.

"Who did you write about?" Jill asked.

"Guess," said Matthew.

"The president?" Jill asked.

Matthew shook his head.

"I hope it wasn't Sally Ride, the astronaut," Emily said.

"St. Patrick," said Matthew. "This month is St. Patrick's Day. March seventeenth."

"That's a great one," said Jill.

"Yes," said Richard. St. Patrick was even better than Stephen what's-his-name.

"Wait till you hear it," said Matthew.

"I have to go to the boys' room," Richard said.

He banged open the door.

If only he had thought of St. Patrick first.

If only he could think of somebody else.

Chapter 8

Richard pulled out his old lion drawing.

He drew a tree next to the lion.

He put new leaves on the tree.

Emily raised her hand. "Can I read my real-person story?"

"It's not due until tomorrow," Ms. Rooney said.

"I'll read it anyway," Emily said.

Ms. Rooney smiled. "All right."

Emily went to the front.

"Sally Ride was the first American woman to go up in space," Emily read.

Richard wished he had more paper. He had forgotten to buy some again.

"Sally's spaceship was called *Challenger*," said Emily.

Richard looked around.

Matthew was playing with the sticks.

Wayne O'Brien was reading a book.

"Sally Ride floated a bag of jelly beans out in space," Emily said.

Matthew stopped playing with the sticks.

Wayne stopped reading.

They both looked at Emily.

"Then," said Emily, "she pulled them back into the *Challenger*. She used a big hook arm."

Richard wondered if Sally Ride had eaten the jelly beans after the flight.

"Very interesting, Emily," said Ms. Vincent.

"Yes," said Ms. Rooney. "Good work."

Ms. Rooney looked up at the clock. "Time for special-help reading," she said.

Richard and Emily and Matthew and Alex went down the hall.

Richard carried his father's old shirt.

He balanced the green-and-orange paper on his head.

At Holly's class he stopped to look in the window.

He stood there waggling his tongue until she looked up. Everyone else was looking too.

Holly's face turned red.

Richard stuck his finger in his nose.

Then he gave Matthew a little punch.

They crossed the hall. They stopped to look out the window.

"The snow pile is almost gone," Matthew said.

"There's a little purple flower on my lawn," Emily said.

Mrs. Paris stuck her head out the door. "Better hurry," she said. "We have a lot to do today."

They went into the reading room.

Richard sat down at the round table.

"Are we going to make kits now?" he asked.

Everyone laughed. Everyone except Mrs. Paris.

"Kites," she said. "Kites for the March wind."

Richard ducked his head.

"You forgot your silent *e*," said Alex. "Kites, not kits."

"Right," said Richard.

He curled up the edge of the green-and-orange-paper package.

He wished he were home.

He wished he were a million skillion miles away from everybody laughing.

"We all make mistakes," said Mrs. Paris. "I'm a terrible kite-maker. I asked Mr. Mancina to come in and help."

Mrs. Paris gave out little balls of string.

The door opened. It was Mr. Mancina.

He was wearing a skinny striped tie.

He twirled it around.

All the special-help readers laughed.

Mr. Mancina picked up two sticks.

He held them in the air.

"Cross one over the other," he said. "Then tie them together in the middle."

Matthew gave Richard two sticks.

"Spread out," said Mrs. Paris.

Richard and Matthew knelt down on the floor.

Richard started to tie his two sticks together.

"The Chinese people love kites," Mr. Mancina said. "They even have a kite day."

He held up his crossed sticks.

He took a ball of string.

He wound the string along the four ends of the sticks. "These are your kite bones," he said.

Richard made kite bones too.

"The Chinese Kite Day is on the ninth day of the ninth month," Mr. Mancina said. He picked up a piece of red paper.

"Now we'll cover the kite bones," he said. "We'll cut the paper so it fits over the whole thing. Then we'll paste the edges on the paper over the string."

Richard looked at his paper.

It was going to make a terrific kite.

It was going to be the best.

"There's an old Chinese story," said Mr. Mancina. "Once upon a time a man had a dream.

He dreamed that something was going to happen to his house."

Mr. Mancina began to cut the red paper.

Richard began to cut his orange-and-green paper too. It was tearing a little bit.

He hoped no one would notice.

Mr. Mancina looked up. "The man took his family away from the house. They flew kites all day."

"Then what?" Emily asked.

"Well," said Mr. Mancina. He folded the red paper around his kite bones. "That night the man found out his house had been destroyed."

"Good thing his family was all right," said Emily.

"Was he a real person?" Richard asked. He wondered if he could use the man for a real-person story.

Mr. Mancina smiled. "It's just an old story, I think. But once a year the Chinese celebrate. They fly kites all day."

Mr. Mancina put some glue around the edges of the kite. He held it in the air.

"Tomorrow," said Mrs. Paris, "we'll put the string on the end of the kites. We'll fly them outside."

Tomorrow, thought Richard. Tomorrow was St. Patrick's Day. He picked up the scissors.

He had to cut a kite tail from his father's blue shirt.

Tomorrow, he thought again. It was the last day for real-people stories.

He had to do something.

Otherwise his report card would be ruined.

Chapter 9

After lunch Richard walked down the hall.

He stopped at the water fountain.

Holly was there ahead of him.

"How come you have to make faces in my classroom window?" she asked. "How come you have to be such a show-off?"

"Listen," Richard said. "I have to ask you something."

Holly wiped some water off her mouth. "What?"

"Can someone get left back twice?" Richard asked.

Holly opened her mouth.

"Can someone get expelled for not doing something?"

"You'd better not," Holly said. "Mommy will be mad as anything."

"I can't help it," Richard said.

Holly shook her frizzy brown hair. "Just my luck to have a brother like you."

Holly looked as if she were going to cry. "I hope my friends don't hear that you're so dumb."

Richard didn't say anything. He guessed he wasn't such a great brother.

He thought about falling into Holly's classroom the other day.

He thought about Holly having to tell everyone that her brother had been left back again.

"It's all your own fault, Richard," Holly said. "You're always forgetting to do what you're supposed to. You're always too lazy."

Richard swallowed.

Holly started to walk away. "I bet you don't even have looseleaf yet."

"I'm getting some today," Richard said. "Right after school."

Holly looked back over her shoulder. "Are you scared?"

Richard nodded.

Holly came back to the water fountain. “What’s the matter, anyway?”

Richard ducked his head. “I can’t find a real person for my real-person story.”

“Is that all?”

“That’s a lot,” Richard said.

“How about George Washington?” Holly asked.

“Noah is—”

“Then James Polk.”

Richard shook his head. “Someone ”

“Tomorrow is St. Patrick’s Day,” said Holly. “How—”

Mrs. Miller stuck her nose out the door. “Young lady. Get back in the classroom.”

Just then Mr. Mancina walked by. “Hi, kids,” he said.

Holly looked at Richard. “How about Mr.—” she began.

Richard opened his eyes wide. He took a quick sip of water.

He squirted a little at Holly.

"Rich . . . ard," Holly said.

Richard raced down the hall.

"Thanks, Holly Polly," he yelled.

He slid into the classroom.

He stopped at Linda Lorca's desk and asked her for a piece of paper.

Then he went back to his seat.

Ms. Rooney had told them to look hard at things.

Too bad he hadn't looked harder at Mr. Mancina.

He closed his eyes for a minute.

Then he began to write.

My real person is Mr. Mancina. He is the principel. He likes Egg McMuffins. He has different kinds of ties like red ones and skinny ones.

Richard looked at his paper. He remembered Mr. Mancina coming into the special-help reading class.

Mr. Mancina buys books for the school. He makes kites. He tells Chinese stories. He is the best.

Richard sat back.

Terrific.

Maybe it was because he was looking hard at Mr. Mancina and didn't even know it.

Just then Ms. Vincent walked by.

She leaned over his shoulder. "That's neat, Richard," she said. "Super."

Ms. Vincent patted him on the shoulder. Then she went to the front of the room.

Matthew looked back at him. "I think we can play ball after school."

"It's almost spring," said Emily. "March is going out like a lamb."

"Can someone lend me some paper?" Richard asked.

Dawn gave him a piece. It had pink flowers on top.

"It's the last time," Richard said. "I'm getting paper today."

"Good," said Dawn.

"I'm going to draw a picture for Holly," Richard said. "Maybe I'll draw a lamb."

"Baaa," said Matthew.

Richard gave him a little poke. "Baaa," he said too.

Then he picked up his crayon.

DATE DU
HIGHSMITH 45-220